To Kathy, Richard and Ted Riley Gascoigne – T. M.

For Rosemary – R. A.

First published in Great Britain by HarperCollins Children's Books in 2012

ISBN 978-0-545-93985-0

12 11 10 9 8 7 6 5 4 3 2 1   15 16 17 18 19 20/0

Printed in the U.S.A.   40

First Scholastic printing, December 2015

THE SOMETHINGOSAUR

Tony Mitton

Illustrated by Russell Ayto

SCHOLASTIC INC.

Long, long ago
in the far mists of time,
deep in the swamps,
in the slush and the slime . . .

Crick, crickle,
crackle . . .

Out comes a leg!

Crick, crickle,
crackle . . .

The shell bursts in two!

What a cute way to say,
"How do you do?"

When it's grown it might shake
the whole swamp with its roar.

But what on earth is it?

A . . .

Something-o-saur . . . ?

Poor little *Something*,
all on his own.
Where is his family?
Is he alone?

Up **stomps** a dinosaur,
huge as they come.

"Hey, great big dinosaur!
Are you my mom?"

"Don't be so silly!
Just look and see.
I'm not your mother.
You're not like me."

Poor little Something,
looking for love.
Oh, could this be Mommy now,
towering above?

"Hey, mega-dinosaur,
are you my ma?
She's got to be somewhere.
She can't have gone far."

"Don't be so silly,

you strange little creature.

Out of my way

or I might have to

EAT YER!"

Off goes our Something.
Where will he roam,
to look for his family,
for love, and for home?

He wanders the deserts,

the swamps,

and the plains.

He travels through blistering heat,

and through rains.

He visits the places
that no dino knows.

And little
by little . . .

he grows . . .

and he **grows.**

He reminds us of something . . .
now what could that be?

If we can be patient,
perhaps we shall see.

Our brave little creature goes on with his quest.
His journey is hard. What a trial and a test!

Then high on a mountain, he spies a strange cave.
Does he dare visit? Is he that brave?

There might be a monster that lurks in its lair!
But it could be his mother who's living up there . . .

To get to the cave
may take quite a long time,
but our brave little creature
sets off on the climb.

Out of the cave comes
a frightening
rumble.

It sounds like the
mountain's beginning to
grumble.

As he climbs closer,
there's smoke and there's heat.
Whatever is Somethingosaur
going to meet?

Then out of the cave comes a . . .

Just look at those teeth
in that jaggedy jaw!

And look at those flames
that come rippling out ...

with trickles of smoke
from that sniffly snout!

But the flames flicker down
and the smoke clears away,
and what's this the monster's
beginning to say?

"Oh, dear little dragon,
my baby, my child,
you've found your way home
through the wastes
and the wild.

You're the egg that I dropped
as I flew through the air,
and I searched and I sought
and I looked EVERYWHERE.

But you've hatched and
you're here and you're
home at your cave.

Oh, dear little dragon,
you're so very brave.
You'll make your Ma proud.
You'll grow sturdy and strong.

Now cuddle up close, 'cause you're where you belong."

And long, long ago, where the dinosaurs roam,
a little lost dragon is happily home.